MARVEL
DOCTOR STRANGE
ATTACK OF THE DOUBT DEMONS

Written by **Liz Marsham**
Illustrated by **Ron Lim** and **Chris Sotomayor**
Based on the Marvel comic book series
Doctor Strange

MARVEL
marvelkids.com

© 2016 MARVEL
All rights reserved. Published by Marvel Press, an imprint of
Disney Book Group. No part of this book may be reproduced
or transmitted in any form or by any means, electronic or
mechanical, including photocopying, recording, or by any
information storage and retrieval system, without written
permission from the publisher. For information address
Marvel Press, 125 West End Avenue, New York, New York 10023.

Printed in the United States of America
First Edition, October 2016
10 9 8 7 6 5 4 3 2 1
ISBN 978-1-4847-8137-1
FAC-029261-16232
Library of Congress Control Number: 2016932825

SUSTAINABLE
FORESTRY
INITIATIVE
Certified Sourcing
www.sfiprogram.org
SFI-01415

In Greenwich Village, New York, sat the Sanctum Sanctorum, home of Doctor Stephen Strange. He was a talented surgeon until a car accident damaged his hands. He searched for a way to mend them. Instead of a cure, he discovered the mystic arts and became the Sorcerer Supreme!

One day, Doctor Strange was consulting the Orb of Agamotto. The Orb was one of his most powerful tools. It showed Doctor Strange people who were in need.

But as he gazed into the glowing Orb, Doctor Strange became confused. It displayed a playground full of children.

"How curious," he said. "None of those children are moving. They're frozen in place!"

Doctor Strange quickly flew to the school. As he approached, he saw teachers rushing toward the playground.

"Stay back!" Doctor Strange called. "Allow me to investigate."

Doctor Strange looked at the playground on the astral plane, where he was able to see things others could not.

Doctor Strange was shocked. Demons had taken over and trapped the children!

The demons had warped the way the playground appeared on the astral plane. Where on the material plane he saw a regular slide, on the astral plane there was a huge twisted slide clouded in darkness. Swings were frozen in a giant block of ice. The jungle gym was now made up of tall spikes with steep drops. And the foursquare court was now a field of flames.

In each of these dangerous areas, the children were afraid to move. And surrounding the children—dancing through the darkness—were the demons.

"By the Hoary Hosts of Hoggoth!" exclaimed Doctor Strange. "Those are doubt demons!"

"Eye of Agamotto, open and reveal the truth to me!" he commanded.

The amulet glowed and showed Doctor Strange an invisible demon flying over the playground. Then he saw a child. She was nervous about asking to join her friends in a game.

The demon noticed the girl's doubt. She froze in fear as it latched onto her. The demon fed on her emotions and grew stronger. Soon it split itself in two.

Other children saw her and became worried. One of her friends came closer. He couldn't see the demon.

The second demon saw its chance. It flew to the boy and latched on. The boy froze. The demons spread, taking over the whole playground!

"It's just as I feared," said Doctor Strange.

He had a difficult task ahead of him. He would have to drive away the doubt demons. And if he doubted himself for even a second, the demons would latch onto him.

Doctor Strange decided to start
by distracting the demons. He stretched
out his hands and flexed his fingers.
"Vapors of Valtorr, cloak these demons
from our sight!" he cried.
Thick mist flowed from his fingers, surrounding
the demons flying around the wooden spikes. They
lost their way and began bumping into each other,
crashing into the jungle gym.

Doctor Strange called out to the children, "You must get to safety! Don't hesitate!"

The children gathered their courage. They climbed down off the jungle gym. By the time the mists cleared, all the children who had been trapped were standing on solid ground.

With a swirl of his Cloak of Levitation, Doctor Strange landed near the field of fire. "I summon the Winds of Watoomb to snuff out these infernal flames!" Suddenly, strong winds whipped across the court.

The blasts of air put out the flames around the children. The doubt demons were not so lucky. The wind picked up the demons and flung them away. Soon the fire was out.

Next, Doctor Strange marched into the
dark cloud. He held out the amulet on his chest.
"May the light of the all-seeing Eye of
Agamotto disperse this blackness!"

Beams of light shot out of his amulet, dissolving the dark clouds.

The beams of light grew brighter, blinding the demons. They howled in pain and retreated into the sky.

"Now!" shouted Doctor Strange. The children on the slide, inspired by the powerful magician, bravely pushed off and slid to safety.

Then Doctor Strange confronted the huge block of ice. He stretched out his hand to touch it and said, "I call on the Flames of the Faltine! Melt this icy prison, but harm not those within!"

Flames sprang from Doctor Strange's hand and licked across the ice. The demons on top of the block retreated from the heat and glided away. Quickly, the mystic fire consumed the ice, until the last group of children was free.

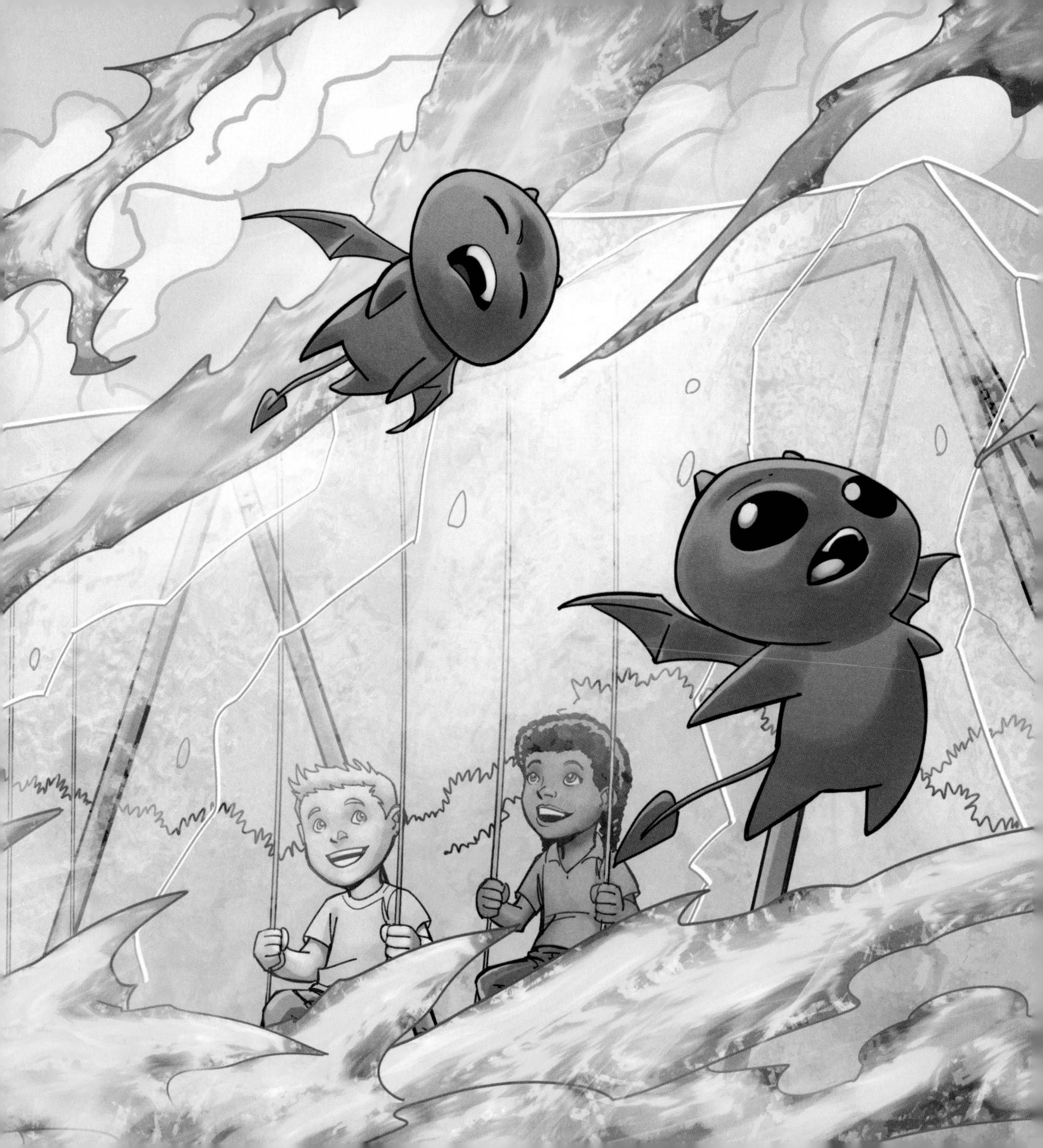

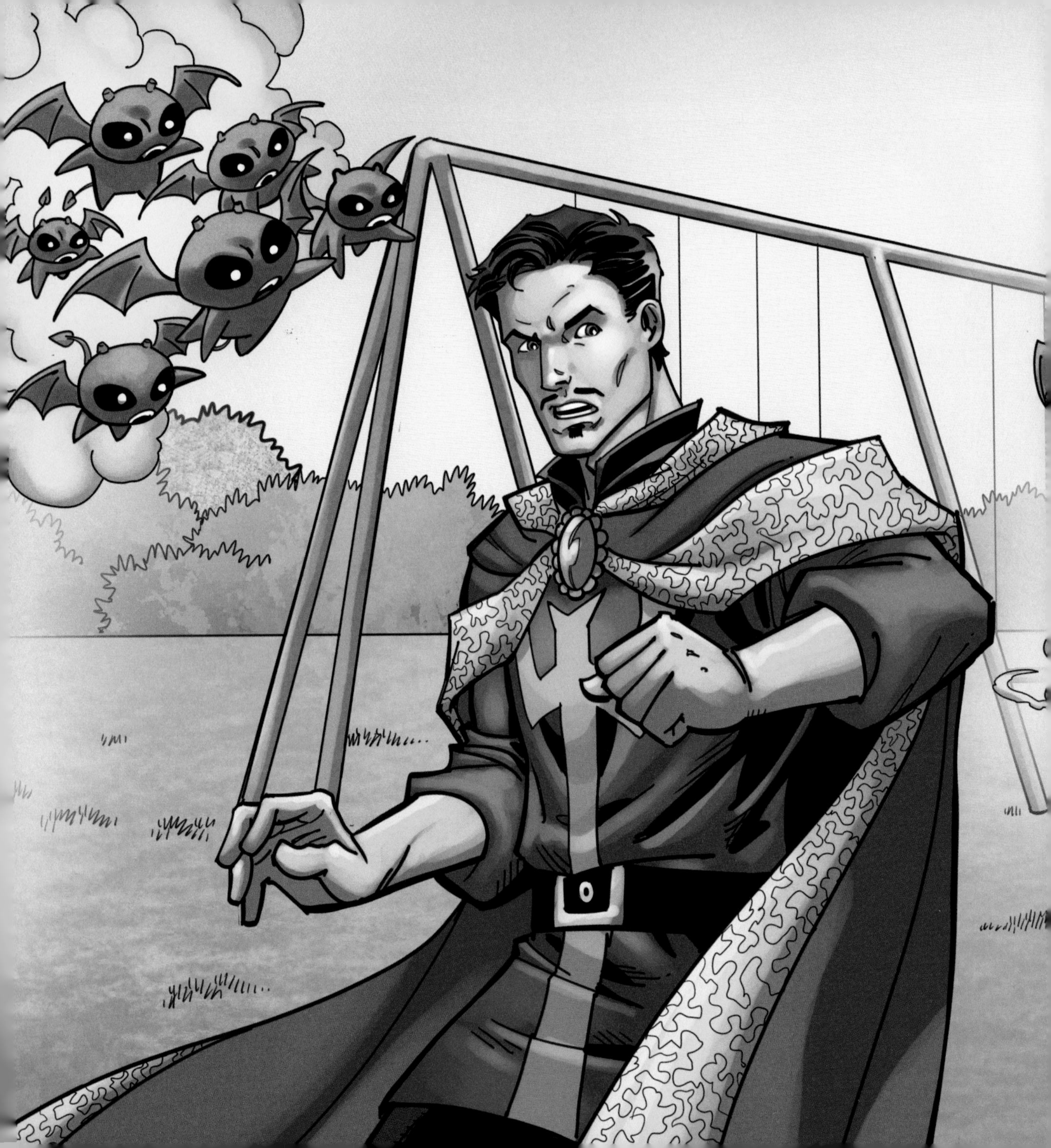

With their victims out of reach, the demons grew angry.
They turned on Doctor Strange. There was no need to stay
hidden. They blinked into sight on the material plane.

The teachers surrounding the playground gasped in fear.
Suddenly, the sky was full of spiky creatures with glowing
eyes! The swarm of demons dove at Doctor Strange.

The demons were closing in on all sides! Doctor Strange muttered a spell under his breath, and a magical ax appeared in his fist.

He swept the shining ax in an arc before him. Demons dodged the blade and pressed in close once more. He swung the ax again and again, nimbly avoiding the ferocious demons every time.

Soon he had cleared a small space around him. It wasn't much, but it would be enough.

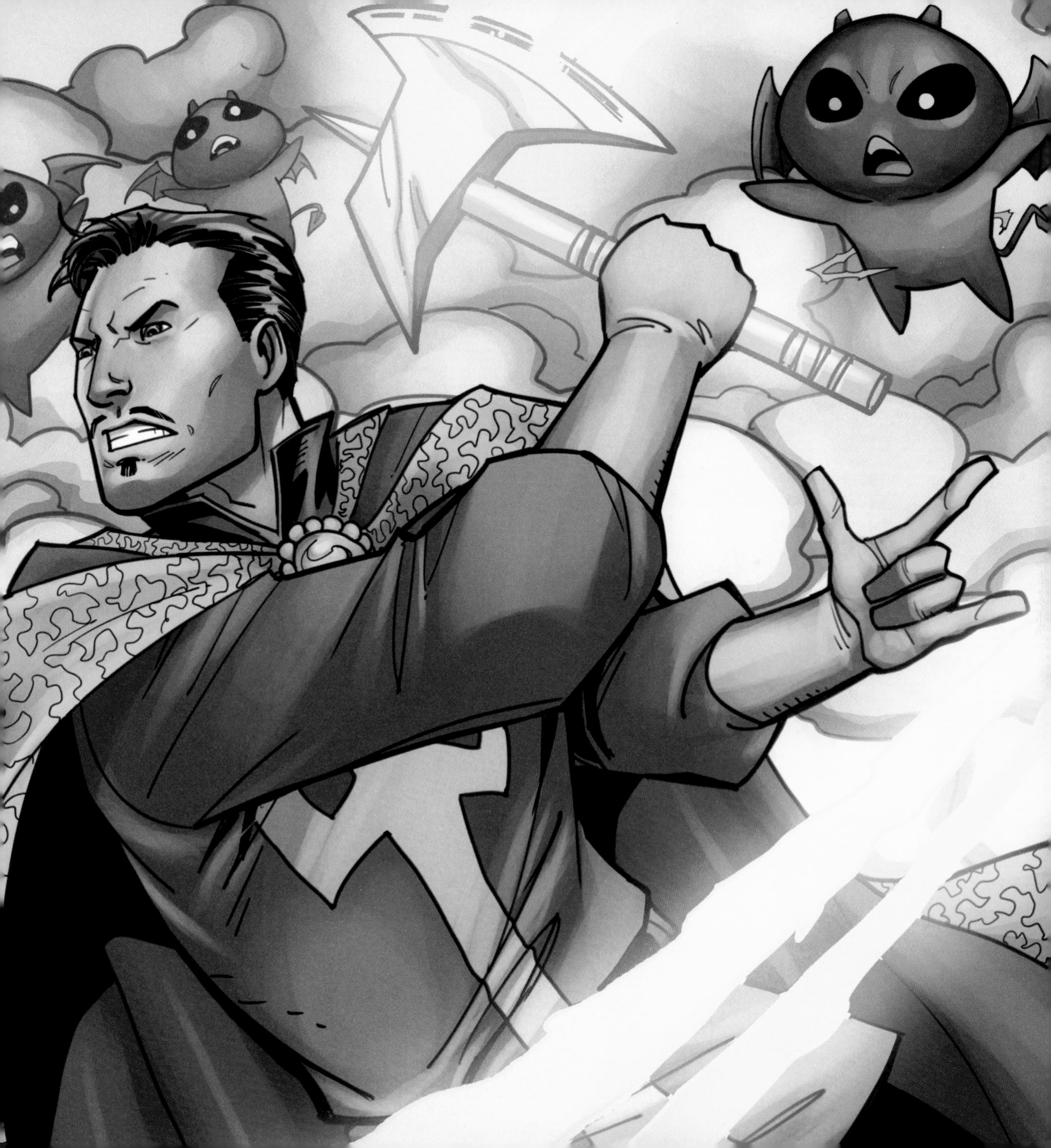

Without a moment's hesitation, Doctor Strange leaped into the air. His Cloak of Levitation knew what he needed, and it shot him up, away from the playground, clear of the swarm.

The enraged doubt demons followed as fast as they could.

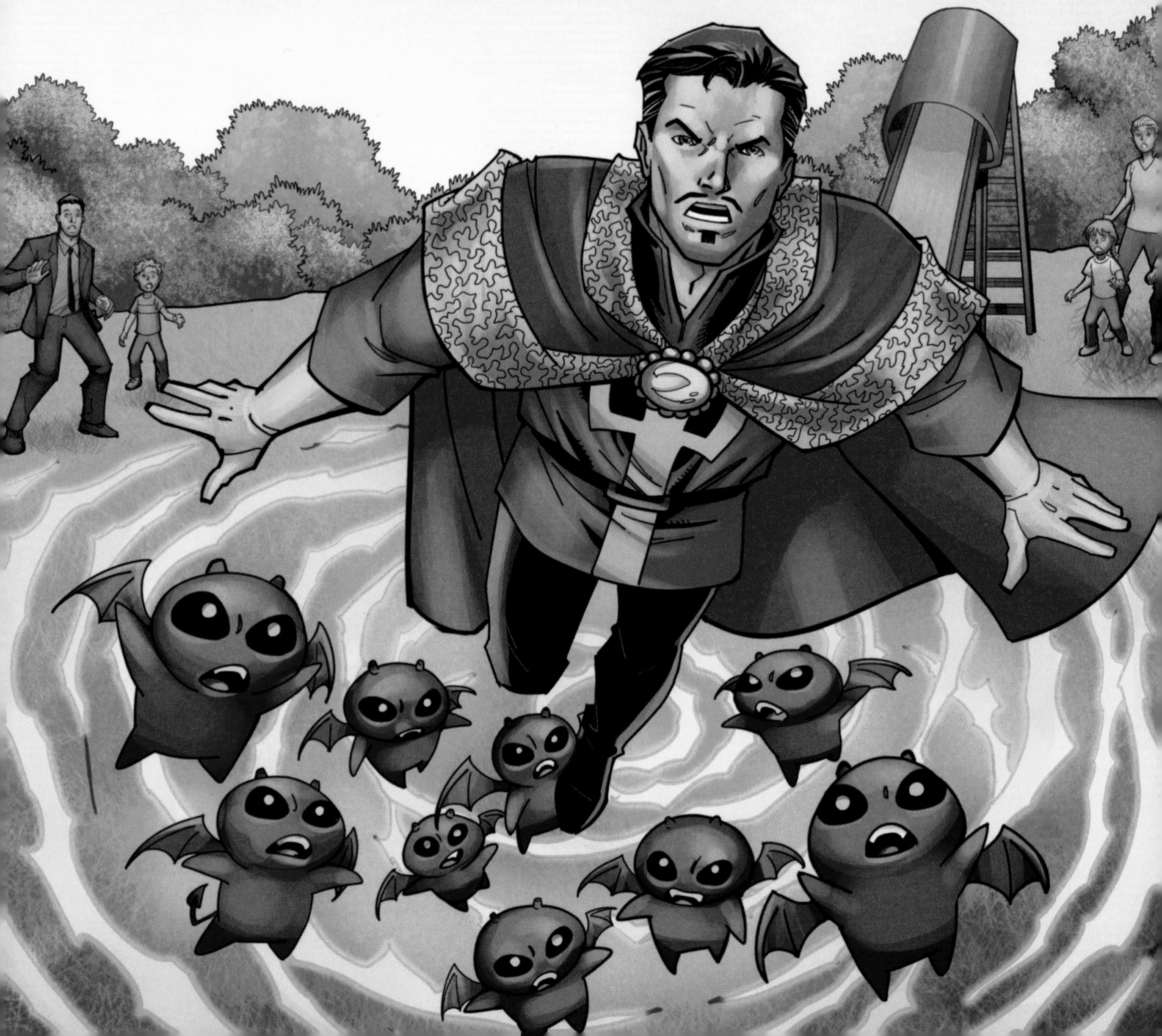

That was exactly what Doctor Strange had been waiting for.

"By the power of the eternal Vishanti, let the Conjurer's Cone drive you from this world! Begone, creatures of darkness!" he proclaimed.

With a crackle and a hiss, the demons were transported to another dimension.

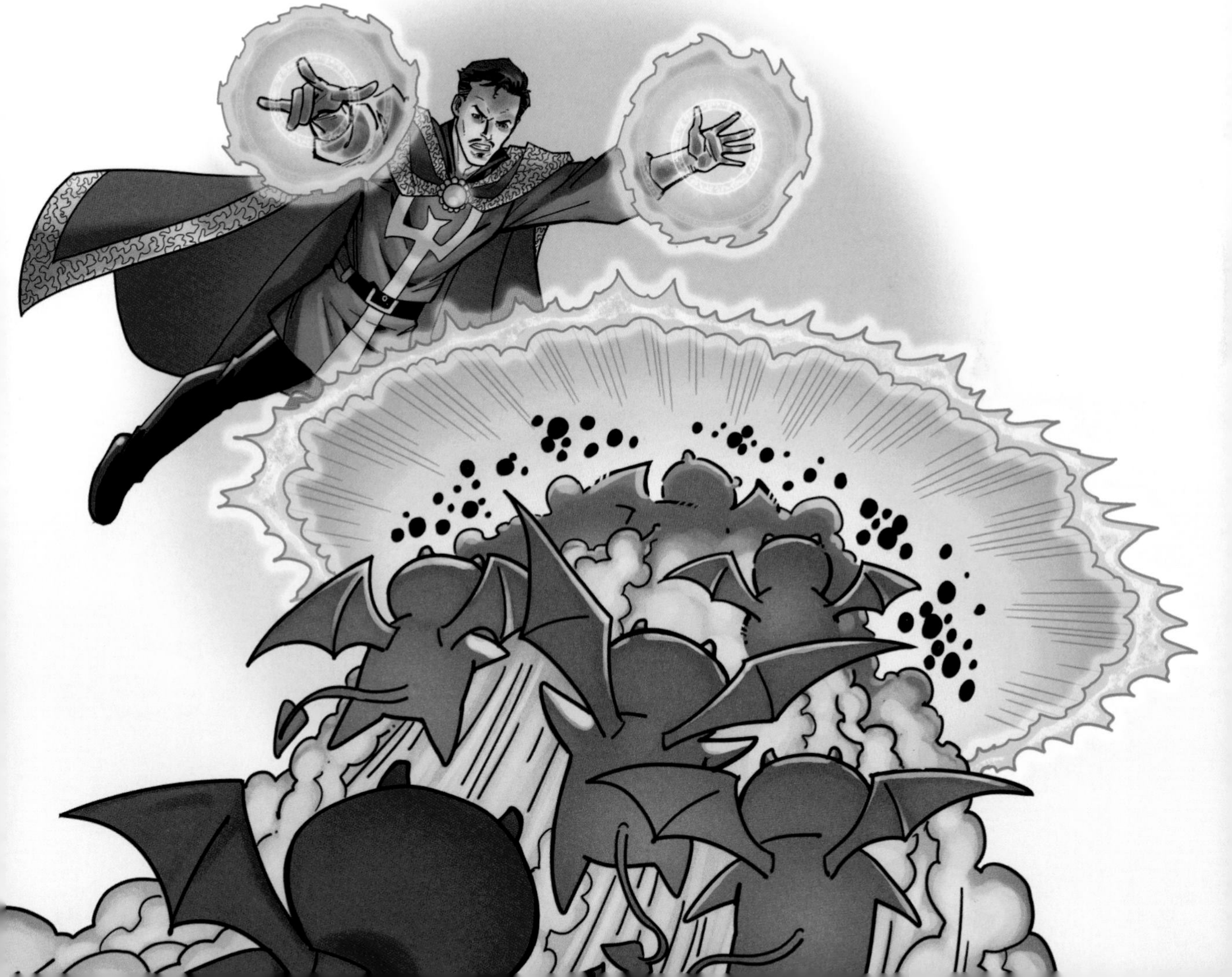

The demons were gone.
The playground was safe.
And all who had witnessed the events said that was the day they learned about the true power of confidence . . . and the many wonderful abilities of Doctor Stephen Strange!